PORCUPINE'S CHRISTMAS BLUES

Jane Breskin Zalben

PHILOMEL BOOKS   New York

Copyright © 1982 by Jane Breskin Zalben
All rights reserved • Published in the
United States by Philomel Books, a division of
The Putnam Publishing Group,
200 Madison Avenue, New York, N.Y. 10016.
Published simultaneously in Canada by
General Publishing Co. Limited, Toronto.
Printed in the United States of America.
Typography by Jane Breskin Zalben

Library of Congress Cataloging in Publication Data
Zalben, Jane Breskin./Porcupine's Christmas blues.
Summary: Lonely and sad at Christmastime, Porcupine
feels better with the support of his friends.
[1. Christmas—Fiction.   2. Friendship—Fiction. 3. Porcupines—
Fiction]   I. Title. / PZ7.Z254Po   1982   [E]   81-20957
ISBN 0-399-20893-3 • AACR2

• To Steven •
When I sing the blues,
you make me feel good about life.

Porcupine was feeling lonely.
The sky was dark.
Winter was outside his window.
Snow dusted the acorn tree in the moonlight.

He strummed on his guitar and sang:

> *I got those Porcupine Blues*
> *running down my quills again.*
> *'Cause my baby left me;*
> *longing for a furry friend.*
> *Come on home, honey,*
> *you're in my thoughts till then.*

He wailed so loudly that he
awakened Bernard and Phoebe Beaver,
who were fast asleep upstairs
under their down-filled quilt.

"What's going on?"
they asked each other.
"Is that Porc jamming until
all hours of the morning again?"
Phoebe nudged Bernard.
"See if something's the matter.

This is the third night this week."
"Phoebe, *you* go, it's your turn."
"I'll choose you," she said. "I have odds."
Bernard put out one paw and lost, as usual.
He still hadn't learned Phoebe always put out
two paws when they played Odds and Evens.

Sleepily, he plodded down to Porcupine.
"What's wrong?" asked Bernard
when Porcupine opened his door.
"Oh, nothing. I'm just sad.
I don't know what it is.
I don't feel at all like Christmas."
"It's okay to feel sad," said Bernard.
"Everybody does, sometimes."
Bernard made himself a chunky peanut
butter and blackberry sandwich.
He offered half to Porc.
"But you have your friends," said Bernard,
"your music that you love, and
a warm place to live."

Bernard lay down on the bed
and crawled under the covers.
"It's true," said Porcupine.
"I have enough food to eat,
and I even have a little extra.
There's a pot of parsley on the windowsill.
The sunshine glowing on me in the afternoon,
and the moon at night. I've got my own pair of
slippers. And there are presents under the tree,
from good friends like you and Phoebe."

Bernard pulled the covers up to his nose.
The ornaments tinkled as the
wind swept under the door. The fire
warmed the inside of the hollow tree.
"Life is good," Porcupine continued.
"You're right, Bernard.
Why should I be sad?"

But Bernard answered with a gentle snore.
He was sound asleep. After listening to
Porcupine all night long, he was tired.

Porcupine picked up his guitar.
He began to play and sing softly:

> *I got those Porcupine highs*
> *way up to the skies.*
> *No blues for me.*
> *Happy as can be.*
> *It's Christmas time*
> *and I'll light the tree.*
> *I have a pal*
> *who is good for me . . .*

"Thanks, Bernard." He tucked the covers
around Bernard. They had fallen off slightly.

Porcupine tiptoed out the door into
the early morning. It was getting light.
His pawprints rested on top of the
snowdrifts. "Good morning," he whispered
to an owl. The owl nodded as Porcupine
chewed some dead branches off the
tree for the owl to use as firewood.

"Merry Christmas," he called to some
squirrels nestled together on a branch
of a large spruce tree. "Come have
some acorn tea with us?" they asked.
"Just a sip, thanks," said Porcupine.
"It's almost time to open the presents."

The sun was coming up.
Porcupine threw a snowball into the air.
He licked some shiny icicles that were
hanging from a cliff. He made a snow sculpture
that looked like Phoebe and Bernard, and rolled
down a hill, where he met another porcupine

who lived across the pond. He invited her to
come for Christmas dinner later that day.
She said she'd love to. Slowly, Porcupine
walked back through the forest, alone,
but not lonely. The blues were gone. He felt
peaceful and happy deep down, at last.

Porcupine went inside the hollow tree.
As he warmed his paws by the fire,
he thought about Christmas dinner.
"Better set another place at the table,"
he said to himself. Then he put a basket
under the tree for Phoebe and Bernard.
It was filled with fresh partridgeberries
that he had picked especially for them.
He put a note in it:

*Thanks for being you. You helped me to
feel better about me. And your being
there when I needed you is the best present
you could have given me.*

Love,
Your Friend Porc

Picking up his guitar, Porcupine smiled
and began to strum "Jingle Bells," very softly.

Christmas had come.